No More

A Sun Ray Community Mystery

By

Susan Raynor Olson

ISBN: 9798863395272

Published by
Heritage Publishing. US
Bradenton, Florida

Dedication

To my son, Derrick Randall Olson. He never expected to see the writing of this mystery or its completion by his mother.

Never underestimate the determination of a woman.

Chapter One

"The Promise"

According to their brochure, the Sun Ray community has all you need to live independently and confidently.

The brochure shows a pastoral and tranquil setting with images of an Olympic-sized, azure swimming pool surrounded by colorful flower beds. It goes on to describe seasonal birds nesting among the abundant greenery. Turtles are sunning on the banks of one of their four large lakes, and ducks are pictured swimming.

After viewing the brochure, I accepted the invitation and moved right into the Sun Ray Independent Living Facility.

Let me introduce myself. My name is Margery Cutter. I'm a retired Dr. of Philosophy.

I looked forward to their promise of elegantly served three-star international cuisine. The award-winning chef was described as creating three delicious meals daily.

Making new friends from a variety of backgrounds and professions was of interest to me.

Becoming a Sun Ray resident also meant no more searching for competent and affordable handymen for constant home repairs, not to mention the continual servicing of the outdoor lighting and confusing electric bills.

No more would I be stuck with the upkeep of the front and back garden. No more would I have to spend money on expensive floral plants requiring constant weeding and watering, lots of watering in the Florida heat.

No more would I have to be on the watch for hidden poison Ivy plants and their itchy and frustrating leaves, ready to reach out and grab me.

No More noisy, nocturnal insects swarming around the deck lights chasing you indoors. You have not lived until such gardening experiences are under your skin.

Over the years, my home symbolized a hyperactive youngster – always in need of attention.

I was glad to be rid of it. At least, that's what I thought.

Chapter Two

"Moving in"

I moved into the Sun Ray Community with the assistance of professional movers, family, and friends. It was chaotic, to say the least. Cardboard boxes were mislabeled, family items and antiques were missing, and furniture was damaged. The chaos would result in days and weeks of copious tears, maybe months before I finally found some of the lost items.

Amid this turmoil of unpacking and searching for lost items, I had my first visitor.

A tall, handsome, seventy-ish male resident knocked at my apartment door. He introduced himself as Henry

Bauerman and suggested welcoming me with cocktails in his suite.

Henry was visibly disappointed when I gracefully declined.

Exhausted from my moving experience had set into every bone of my tired body. I wanted to sleep forever in my apartment's unmade bed.

Perhaps a "Do not disturb" sign on the door would communicate to other well-meaning residents my unavailability.

Some days later, I finally stirred. Looking out of my spacious apartment windows, I saw a mammoth wooden crate being delivered. It reminded me of a museum container for something valuable. I wondered what expensive item could be enclosed inside the crate and which resident the crate could be destined for.

Chapter Three

"The Awareness"

Meeting Henry while checking for my mail in the mail room, he again invited me to his suite, this time for dinner.

Curiosity got the better of me, and I accepted.

We were served by his part-time butler and indulged in French champagne in ultra-fine crystal glasses from Germany. Images of exotic birds and butterflies from South America graced the exquisite hand-painted china plates that took my breath away. They were too beautiful to use for food, I thought.

To complete the mood of the evening, Henry wore a black and white tweed jacket with a red ascot. Did men still wear ascots? I wondered.

The overall effect of Henry's dinner in suite #833 was overwhelming and memorable.

I gazed around the room and noticed a spectacular red velvet couch.

Noting my interest in the twenty-five-piece chandelier above our heads, he told me it was imported from Venice, Italy. As we walked around his apartment, he proudly told me more, explaining that he recently had the entire kitchen redone with cutting-edge appliances and marble countertops installed. It hardly looked used.

I did admire his artwork by English artist J. M. W. Turner, alongside paintings by famous Hudson Valley artists.

On visiting the ladies' room, the decor was over the top with displays of Matisse paintings.

Passing Henry's masculine study, lined with cherry bookcases filled with art pieces and rare books, I saw the massive wooden crate I had previously seen from my window.

As Henry talked, I listened carefully to learn more about Henry. He boasted of his wealth and his status as a Forbes 500 millionaire. He claimed his investments included a successful stock portfolio and an import/export business.

Not only did he like to talk about himself, but also about women non-stop.

I was not surprised. Henry loved women, all women. The word circulating among the female residents was Henry's search for wife number three. He was a bit of a Cassanova.

Throughout the evening, Henry exhibited inappropriate behavior towards me. I had a hard time keeping his hands off my body. I'm not a prude, but there is a time and place, and this was not it. I hardly knew the man.

There was only one solution to his obscene overtures. I feigned a headache and exited for the evening.

I would have loved to see what the crate contained, but that would have to wait for another day.

Chapter Four

"Community Dining"

Dining with several new acquaintances one evening, Henry inevitably joined our table. My dinner companions were all attractive single female residents.

Our server for the evening was Emilia, a young, pretty Latino girl in her early twenties.

I observed Henry's rather frisky behavior towards Emilia while the young lady in question merely giggled as Henry continued his apparent, amorous behavior.

The ladies at the table found his public display of groping inappropriate, as did I.

When a couple of the ladies voiced their opinion of his actions, he brushed their remarks aside. "Just having a bit of fun," Henry said gayly.

Chapter Five

"Love in a Box"

Waiting in the elegant lobby for our table to be ready, we saw a small box tied with satin ribbons left at our dining table with Emilia's name on the tag.

Emilia opened the opened the box. Excitement and surprise were etched on her face.

We all tried to guess what might be inside the carefully wrapped box.

She pulled out a note from her sugar daddy, Henry. Then we saw his gift—a beautiful silver bracelet with large royal blue gems.

Emilia was delighted and ran to Henry, giving him several hugs. Henry responded with his own loving embrace. Obviously, Emilia loved her stunning silver and royal blue bracelet, blissfully unaware of Henry's true motive or intentions.

Chapter Six
"Juicy Gossip"

A few days later, I was surprised to receive an invitation to meet Henry's two ex-wives for coffee in the Wicker Lounge of the Sun Ray Community Center. Why me, I wondered.

Entering the room, I saw two ladies I had not seen before. They waved me over to their table.

The first to speak introduced herself, "Hello, I'm Margaret Bauerman, wife number one." She reached to shake my hand while sitting in a motorized wheelchair.

"Henry divorced me shortly after a fall left me in this damn thing."

The other woman stood to reach across the table. She was tall and attractive. "I'm wife number two. Felicity Stuart. I divorced the bastard when I was tired of his philandering and playing around.

We talked briefly, and I discovered that Margaret was an internationally known retired musician. Felicity had retired from an exciting career in the FBI. I enjoyed getting to know such intelligent and accomplished women.

Getting to the subject of our meeting, we intimately discussed Henry's relationship with Emilia. It had become community gossip spread by all the female residents that Henry was searching for wife number three.

I was surprised to learn something extraordinary and unexpected. If Henry married a third time, his will would automatically remove both ex-wives.

Felicity had found this out from an old acquaintance and told Margaret. The exes were understandably upset with Henry's new will. They didn't say to Margery Cutter that they were planning to stop Henry for his idea of cutting them out of his will, no matter what.

We all wondered why Emilia delighted in Henry's sexual advances. The only answer we came up with was money.

Chapter Seven
"Another Thrill"

As we took our places for dinner the following evening, we couldn't help but notice a new gift meant for Emilia.

I thought it odd that she would receive these gifts in such a public manner.

As Emilia came to our table to serve us, she found the gift addressed to her. Everyone in the dining room and a young waiter, Sebastian, heard her squeals of delight when she opened the box.

Henry beamed with delight as he placed a breathtaking silver and royal blue necklace around her delicate neck.

Chapter Eight
"Showing Off the Glitz"

A dance party planned at the Sun Ray Community Center would be a treat for the residents and staff alike. A benefactor had arranged for everyone to be able to attend, including the staff.

I couldn't help wondering if this was Henry's way of showing off his gifts. Emilia did look amazing. Several residents commented on her blue silk party dress that showed off her stunning jewelry set to perfection.

Henry and Emilia strolled around the room, arm in arm. Was Henry publicly announcing Emilia as his new young lover?

I saw Sebastian leaning against a wall, glaring at Henry and Emilia. From the longing looks he had thrown Emilia, I knew he was enamored of her. He was a struggling college student and could not compete with Henry and his extravagant gifts.

Chapter Nine
"Getting Even"

The following evening, our little group had gathered for dinner. It seemed that Henry was to be a permanent part of our all-female entourage.

There were six of us sitting around the table, including Henry; Mrs. McCafferty, a retired high school teacher; Miss Laughton, a librarian from Michigan; Mrs. Brigham, who clerked for a judge, a fascinating woman named Pasha something from India; I can't pronounce her last name and myself.

From where I was sitting, I could see Emilia and Sebastian at the salad station in the kitchen. They were laughing and preparing the individual salads.

I watched them put together the leafy lettuce and chunky feta cheese. Sebastian added raspberries, blueberries, blackberries, and strawberries. Emilia then dressed the colorful salad with poppyseed dressing before bringing it out to the guests.

Sebastian placed Henry's salad before him. Henry scowled at Sebastion. He was not eager to eat his favorite salad. He gazed across the table at Emilia, imagining her in his kingsized bed.

Smiling at Emilia, Henry consumed his salad.

I saw Henry reach for his wine glass, and a strange look came across his face. His eyes glazed over, and he grabbed the tablecloth, pulling it to the floor as he fell, taking china, glasses, and dinnerware with him.

Henry lay weak and gasping among the shattered glass and china.

The room was chaotic as residents screamed, and Emilia ran to Henry's side.

One of the residents, a retired doctor, tried to help, but CPR proved useless. Henry was dead.

The emergency services arrived shortly, confirming what we already knew, and closed Henry's staring eyes.

Questions danced in my head. Was there a respiratory problem that caused Henry to stop breathing?

Did Henry have a heart condition? Did he choke on a bit of salad?

These questions and more were for the police if anything suspicious turned up in the postmortem.

In either case, the result was the same. Henry was dead.

Chapter Ten

"The Investigation Begins"

Lieutenant Schofield from the Police Department and his team showed up and added to the chaos.

Photos were taken from all angles. Evidence was gathered and taken away.

Our little dining group had our pictures taken, along with our information. I did not appreciate the thought of a lineup including me and the other residents.

After removing Henry's body, the lieutenant would not allow the staff to clean up the mess remaining on the floor.

"I'll let you know. Right now, it's all evidence."

Dinner ended abruptly, with no one wanting to sit and finish their three-course meal, whether someone had just died suspiciously or not. The residents retreated to their rooms and locked their doors. Late-night delivery orders were the norm that evening.

Chapter Eleven
"The Discovery?"

A night of restless sleep, tossing and turning, prevented me from waking up early.

I sat with my morning coffee, looking out over the pond and watching the ducks skimming over the still surface. I pondered the cause of Henry's death. Was it murder at the Sun Ray Community? Yet, no one discovered any visible outpouring of blood or open wound on Henry's body. My fingers drummed on the table, thinking of another possibility.

A knock on my door disturbed my thinking. Pasha came to tell me the police were back and wanted everyone from Henry's table and the dining room servers immediately.

Lieutenant Scholfield separated us, and we were each asked the following questions.

"How well did you know the deceased?

"Were you aware of his import/export business?"

"Did you know how he accumulated his wealth?"

"What did you know about his relationship with his two ex-wives?"

"Have you been in Henry's suite?"

"What was Henry's relationship with the staff like?"

After that round of questions, the police took a break to compare answers. We were not allowed to speak to each other.

I overheard that the police conducted a thorough search of Henry's suite. Hushed voices told me the large wooden crate was the most apparent discovery.

I had to scoot my chair closer to hear the rest.

Inside the crate, they found artwork by Titian and Botticelli and jewelry. Paperwork and documents found in the chest indicated the art was stolen and the jewelry was from wealthy Jewish families. The records date to the time of the Nazi occupation of Germany.

My hand flew to my mouth to silence a gasp of surprise. I knew Henry was a scoundrel but a Nazi? Something wasn't right. Henry was too young to be a Nazi. There had to be another explanation. Where did the crate come from?

An art appraiser was called in to authenticate and value the pieces. The police also asked for a jewelry expert to value the jewelry.

If Henry had managed to submit his stolen Nazi loot to Christie's or Sotheby's auction houses, it would have meant a substantial increase in the bottom line of his import/export business.

After a short lunch, the questioning was to begin again. I was getting tired of this.

Before the interrogation started, Luitenant Scholfield stood in the middle of the room.

" A postmortem was performed, and it was discovered that Henry Bauerman was poisoned. The substance was found in something he ate that evening. His stomach contents were analyzed, and the poison was belladonna. The coroner tells me it's part of the Deadly Nightshade family. Its fruit would look very much like a blueberry when ripe. Mr. Bauerman would not have known the difference. I'm told it would only take two – five berries to be lethal.

Someone in this room killed Henry Bauerman.

Chapter Twelve

"Who Done in Henry?"

One of Lieutenant Scholfield's officers came up, whispered something in his ear, and handed him a folder.

Schofield looked over at where Emilia and Sebastian were sitting. Sebastian took off like a rocket as officers began moving in that direction.

After a minor scuffle in the lobby, they returned with Sebastian in handcuffs.

The forensics team had found Sebastian's fingerprints on the outside of Henry's salad bowl and a small empty container in the kitchen. The kitchen and wait staff are to wear gloves when preparing and serving the meals for the residents.

It suddenly dawned on me that Sebastian was not wearing gloves the evening Henry died. Something any good murderer should know.

Sebastian was in tears, confessing his guilt and love for Emilia.

He explained how jealously made him do it. He could not afford the expensive gifts and elaborate lifestyle of Emilia's sugar daddy, Henry. Sebastian hated watching Henry's lude sexual advances towards Emilia.

"You only loved Henry's money. It was my dream to make you happy forever with me. I wanted to marry you."

It was not to be as we watched the police take Sebastian away.

Chapter Thirteen

"Tying up Loose Ends"

I had one burning question that was yet to be answered. I paid a visit to Lieutenant Scholfield's Office the following week.

I sat across the desk from the lieutenant. I asked, "How did Mr. Bauerman come into possession of stolen artwork and jewelry reportedly taken out of Berlin, Germany, before and during the Second World War? His age doesn't work with the timeline."

"We had to do a lot of digging to come up with that answer," The lieutenant said. "You told us you saw the crate being delivered. Apparently, Mr. Bauerman was left the chest in his father's will some years ago. Bauerman's father was from Berlin, Germany, and immigrated here after the war. He was also in the import/export business."

"Why did the crate only turn up now?" I had to know.

"Henry Bauerman's business was not doing as well as it used to, and paying the Sun Ray Community Center fee was draining his bank accounts. He had to try to sell his father's stolen goods.

"I imagine buying Emilia expensive gifts didn't help."

"You've got that right. Well, good day, Mrs. Cutter. I hope your time at the Sun Ray Community Center is less exciting but pleasant."

"Thank you, lieutenant. Only time will tell."

The work of the Monuments Men inspired this short story.

Art historian Lynn H. Nicholas wrote,
"Without the Monuments Men, a lot of the most important treasures of European culture would be lost," Nicholas says. "They did an extraordinary amount of work protecting and securing these things."

Walker Hancock, Lamont Moore, George Stout, and two unidentified soldiers in Marburg, Germany, June 1945.

Thomas Carr Howe papers, Archives of American Art

https://www.smithsonianmag.com/history/true-story-monuments-men-180949569/

Acknowledgments

Writing the mystery No More, dear reader, has been somewhat akin to cooking a dinner for 10 People - lots of coordination.

Time deadlines to prevent overcooked food, challenges of ingredients, and utter exhaustion when finished.

At this imaginary elaborate dinner are very special guests.

I am grateful for the advice and creativity of fellow author Brenda Spalding.

No More would not be printed without the technical support of Coleen Greytak. Stretch Webber gave editing advice.

Also important was the encouragement from family and friends, including Aris Efthimides and Donna Pickard.

To all who were partners in No More, thank you.

You may be in my will.

Cover Photo 27203056 | Ducks Pond © Jolita Marcinkene | Dreamstime.com

About the Author

Author of Quinn's Discovery Series
for children
Quinn's Beautiful Tree
Quinn's Camping Adventure
Quinn at the Beach
Quinn Goes to the Circus
Quinn at the Museum

Susan Raynor Olson, PhD is from upstate New York and now resides in Florida. She is a graduate of Rollins College, University of Georgia, and The Ohio State University. In addition to her higher education experience teaching Communications, Susan Co-Founded GIVING MATTERS. A philanthropic initiative for women making a difference. SITTING PRETTY is a fashion company she formed for designing easy to wear fabrics. Her passions are grandsons Quinn and Graham, international travel, gardening, and reading.

Contact the author – olsonsusan89@gmail.com

Made in the USA
Columbia, SC
18 November 2023

26479513R00022